For my father, Hugh Antonsen

©1985 by Ruth Brown.
First published in 1985 by Andersen Press Ltd., 19–21 Conway Street,
London W.1. Published in Australia by Hutchinson Publishing Group
(Australia) Pty. Ltd., Melbourne, Victoria 3122. All rights reserved.
Colour separated by Photolitho Offsetreproduktionen AG, Zürich, Switzerland.
Printed in Italy by Grafiche AZ, Verona.

British Library Cataloguing in Publication Data
Brown, Ruth
  The big sneeze.
  I. Title
  823'.914 [J] PZ7
  ISBN 0-86264-088-1

THE BIG SNEEZE
Ruth Brown

Andersen Press London
Hutchinson of Australia

One hot afternoon, the farmer and
his animals were dozing in the barn. The
only sound was the buzz-buzz of a lazy fly.

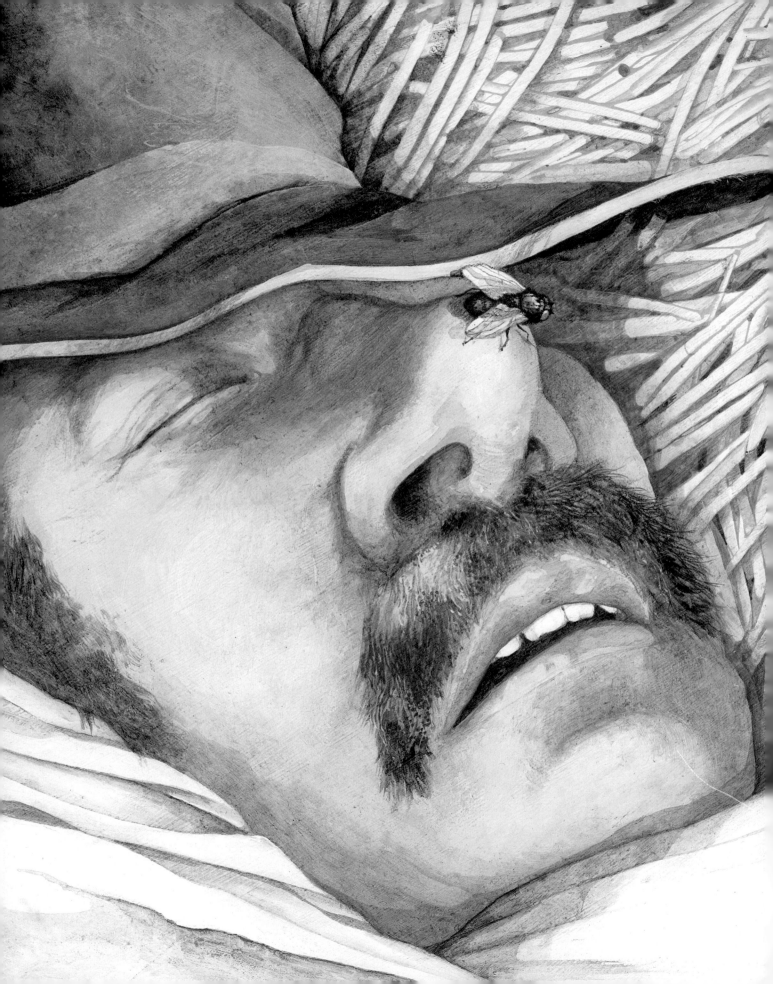

Suddenly the buzzing stopped –
the fly had landed right on the end of the farmer's nose!

"ATISHOOOOOOOOOOO!" the farmer sneezed so hard
that the fly was blown high up into a spider's web.

This disturbed the spider,
who captured the fly –

which alerted the sparrow,
who chased the spider.

This wakened the cat,
who leapt at the bird —

which woke the dog,
and frightened the rats –

who fled from the barn,
chased by the dog –

which scattered the startled
hens from their roost —

and panicked the terrified donkey!

"What on earth have you done?" shrieked the farmer's wife.

"Nothing, my dear," replied the farmer. "I only sneezed!"